A HAPPY BOOK
OF
HAPPY STORIES

BOOKS BY WILLIAM J. LEDERER

The Ugly American (with Eugene Burdick)
A Nation of Sheep
All the Ship's at Sea
Ensign O'Toole and Me
Timothy's Song
The Story of Pink Jade
The Last Cruise
Sarkhan, Reissued as *The Deceptive American*, (with Eugene Burdick)
Our Own Worst Enemy
Spare-Time Article Writing for Money
Complete Cross-Country Skiing and Ski Touring
(with Joe Pete Wilson)
The Mirages of Marriage (with Don D. Jackson)
Marital Choices
Marriage for and against
(contributor)

W · W · NORTON & COMPANY · NEW YORK · LONDON

A HAPPY BOOK
OF
HAPPY STORIES

by

WILLIAM J. LEDERER

———————

This book was designed by Antonina Krass
Display type is Bernhard Modern Roman
Text type is V.I.P. Garamond
Manufactured by Vail-Ballou Press, Inc.

Library of Congress Cataloging in Publication Data

Lederer, William J., 1912–
A happy book of happy stories.

1. Christmas stories.   I. Title.
PS3562.E3H3 1981   813'.54   81–9574
ISBN 0-393-01414-2   AACR2

W. W. Norton & Company, Inc. 500 Fifth Avenue, New York N.Y. 10110
W. W. Norton & Company Ltd. 25 New Street Square, London EC4A 3NT

1 2 3 4 5 6 7 8 9 0

To E.H.S. who participated
in these stories

CONTENTS

PREFACE · 9

IS THERE A SANTA CLAUS? · 11

A CHRISTMAS BALLAD FOR THE CAPTAIN · 15

THE CHRISTMAS MIRACLE AT ELCARIM · 27

A SAILOR'S GIFT · 37

TIMOTHY'S SONG · 43

IS THERE A SANTA CLAUS? · 57

PREFACE

All the events in this book took place at Christmas. However, the stories are for all seasons. Christmas, as you will find out, comes every day of the year—that is, if you will allow it. But what is Christmas?

The Yuletide, in Christian cultures, celebrates the birth of Jesus. However, almost all peoples of the Northern Hemisphere (and some in the Southern) rejoice at the time of the winter solstice—which is the time of Christmas. Long before Jesus, people were joy-filled at the end of December because—among other things—it is the moment when the days become longer and the dark, cold nights begin shortening. It is a symbol of soon-to-come spring. It is a symbol of the rebirth of all living things.

This happy occasion takes place everywhere, as you will see. The stories reported in this book occurred in diverse places—on an isolated island, in an airport, in a Navy ship, in the slums of New York, in a French restaurant, and in church. Some of the characters are old people, some are children, some are middle-aged, and some are animals. Every story concerns someone who has discovered the joy of being alive, which, of course, is what Christmas is all about. This is a book for children, for young adults, for old people, middle-aged people, and for animals.

It is called, *A Happy Book of Happy Stories.*

There simply is no other title so appropriate.

IS THERE
A SANTA
CLAUS?

This event occurred when I was stationed in Hawaii.

Near us lived a large Samoan family—mother, father, nine children, and several uncles and aunts. The mother worked for us as a combination maid, cook, and a general fixer-upper of anything that went wrong. However, by employing the mother, we also acquired the nine children. There was no predicting when some or all of them might accompany their mother to our house.

Once—in mid-December—as I was about to go on a business trip to New York, the entire family was at our house. As I said good-bye, I told all the children (including my three) to be good—to thus make certain that Santa Claus would bring them presents at Christmas.

The eight-year-old Samoan girl (her name was Lanikai) said, "Bill, is there really a Santa Claus?"

"Indeed, Lanikai, of course there's a Santa Claus."

The fifteen-year-old Samoan boy said, "Oh, yeah! How do you know there's a Santa Claus?"

"Well, er. . . ."

"Yes," said a whole tribe of Samoan children (along with my three boys), "how do you know there's a Santa Claus?"

My wife looked at the clock and said, "If you don't leave now, you'll miss your plane."

The tribe shouted, "What about Santa Claus?"

*"Look, kids," I said, "I'm late. But I promise you that
when I come back just before Christmas, I'll tell you how it
is I* know *there's a Santa Claus."*

"Promise?"

"Yes, I promise."

With that I drove to the airport.

*On my trip, I dug into my memory for every experience
I'd ever had concerning the* real *Santa Claus. Deep within
me I knew that the legend of Santa Claus was more than a
dream, more than a fantasy used by parents to entertain
their children. I knew that Santa Claus was real.*

*But how could I convince the children? With parables?
With eyewitness accounts?*

*During my two weeks of traveling, I made notes on all
the thoughts I had on the subject. From these notes I recalled
some of the stories and accounts which follow.*

To the first account, I was a witness.

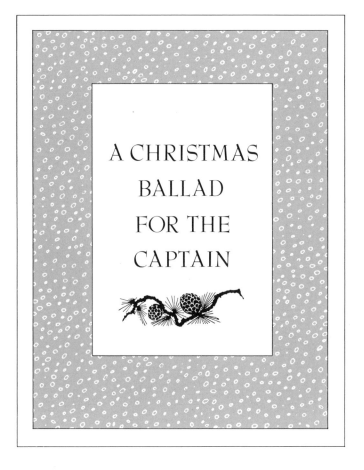

A CHRISTMAS BALLAD FOR THE CAPTAIN

I was the executive officer of the Navy destroyer in which the events of this story took place. It was in the early months of World War II. The rapidly expanding U.S. Navy desperately was seeking trained personnel to man the hundreds of new ships which were being built. The Navy took whoever was available—even the inmates of naval prisons.

There are five major characters in the story. One was our commanding officer—a very shy man who has requested that his real name not be used. The other four have no objections to being identified, and their real names are used.

Also, the names of the motion picture stars are real. They were stars forty years ago. Some of the young people reading this book might not be familiar with these stars. But, take my word for it, they were glamorous, beautiful, and, at that time, among the most famous people in the world.

I did not write this story. One of the men in our ship wrote it shortly after our ship was torpedoed and sunk on the way back from Anzio. He sent it to me and asked me to edit it, which I have done. His reason for writing the story was to send it to all surviving members of our ship as a small Christmas present.

After editing it, and revising it somewhat, I returned his manuscript. It appears in this book in the author's final revision—the way it was when he sent it to me on the following Christmas.

A CHRISTMAS BALLAD FOR THE CAPTAIN

 Captain Elias Stark, commanding officer of our destroyer, was a square-shouldered New Hampshire-man, as quiet and austere as the granite mountains of his native state. About the only time the enlisted men heard him talk was when they reported aboard for the first time. He would invite them to his cabin for a one-minute speech of welcome, then question them about their families, and note, with pen and ink, the names and addresses of the sailors' next of kin.

That was the way he had first met the "Unholy K's"—Krakow, Kratch, Koenig, and Kelly. They had arrived with a draft of seventeen men from the naval prison at Portsmouth. Most of the prison group were bad eggs, but the worst were these four sailors from a small coal mining town in Pennsylvania. They had chests and shoulders like buffaloes, fists like sledgehammers, black stubble beards, and manners to match.

They had once been good kids, the mainstays of St. Stephen's choir in their hometown, but somehow they had gone astray. They seemed to specialize in getting into trouble together, as a quartet. All four went into the navy direct from reform school. Within six months they were in serious trouble again and had been sent to Portsmouth Naval Prison.

When they were called to the captain's cabin, they listened to his welcome speech with exaggerated expressions of boredom. Then the Old Man broke out his record book to note the names and addresses of the sailors' next of kin. He looked up inquiringly.

Krakow, the leader of the Unholy K's, took the initiative. Spreading his tremendous arms, he pulled Kelly, Kratch, and Koenig into a tight circle. "The four of us, sir, ain't got no family. We ain't got parents or wives or relatives." He paused. "All we got is girl friends, eh, fellas?"

Captain Stark simply puffed on his pipe. Patiently he asked, "Would you give me your best ladies' names and addresses for our records?"

The Unholy K's glanced at one another. Krakow said, "Sir, we don't feel like it's an officer's business who our girls are." He stopped as Kelly tugged his sleeve and whispered to him.

"Okay," continued Krakow sarcastically, "you want to know who our best girls are, I'll tell you. Mine's Rita Hayworth, Kelly's is Ginger Rogers, Kratch's is Lana Turner, and Koenig's is Paulette Goddard. They all got the same address: Hollywood, *sir.*"

"Very well," said the captain, "I will list those ladies' names in my records. Thank you, that will be all."

As soon as the Unholy K's got belowdecks they began bragging how they had made a fool out of the Old Man. Kelly started a bawdy song, and Krakow, Kratch, and Koenig joined in. Each man, in turn, made up a lyric while the other three harmonized. They had splendid voices, and with their choirboy training they formed a wonderful quartet. They sang four unprintable verses about the captain and why he wanted their girls' addresses.

Actually the captain had a good reason for obtaining personal information about the men. He strongly believed it was his duty to keep their families informed on how they were getting along. So, once every three months, in blunt New England fashion, he sent a personal note written in tiny, neat hand to everyone's next of kin.

For example:

> Dear Madam,
>
> Your son John is well—and as happy as can be expected in North Atlantic gales. If he shaved more often and cleaned his clothes more meticulously he would be more popular with his division chief.
>
> I think highly of him as a gunner's mate and, with luck, you should see him in a few months. You will find he has put on 12 pounds, and the extra flesh hangs well on him.
>
> Sincerely,
> Elias Stark
> Commander, U.S. Navy

In September, after a year in the combat zone, our destroyer went to the Brooklyn Navy Yard for a three-week overhaul. Almost all the officers and men went home on furloughs. Only the Old Man stayed on board the entire time, working alone, day and night. No one knew the nature of his apparently urgent business; but whenever we passed his cabin we saw him hunched over his desk, scratching away with an old-fashioned pen, while his cherrywood pipe sent up clouds of blue smoke.

We were puzzled also by the scores of parcels in plain wrappers that began coming to the Old Man before we sailed. It was not until much later that we found out what they contained.

Meanwhile, our destroyer had gone to sea again, protecting convoys through the North Atlantic to England. It was rough work. Icy gales battered us; ships were torpedoed almost every night. We had little sleep, and much physical discomfort. Everyone drooped with fatigue. Tempers became edgy, and there were fights. Captain Stark was constantly on the bridge, smoking his pipe and watching everything carefully. Despite the fact that his clear blue eyes became bloodshot from exhaustion and he stooped a bit from weariness, he remained calm and aloof.

If he knew how the Unholy K's were trying to destroy the ship's morale, he never mentioned it. It was their well-rendered ballads that did the dirty work. Everyone was afraid of these four bullies; but when they sang their insidious songs about the ship's officers, the crew listened. Their lyrics were so catchy that a song rendered in the aftercrew's washroom would be repeated all over the ship within a half-hour. No officers ever heard the four men sing; but the results of their music were uncomfortably apparent.

The Unholy K's had one song about the hundreds of packages which the captain had locked in the forward peak tank. The lyrics said that the boxes contained silk stockings, cigarettes, whiskey, drugs, and other black-market goods which the captain was going to sell in England. They depicted the captain becoming a millionaire and retiring to a mansion in New Hampshire as soon as the war was over.

The crew began to ask questions: Why *should* the Old Man be hiding the parcels? Why *had* they been delivered with so much secrecy? It was even rumored that the Old Man was head of a black-market cartel and the cartons contained drugs stolen from navy supply depots. But when the crew saw Captain Stark, tall, quiet, dignified, they knew in their hearts that the rumors were impossible.

In mid-December we shoved off from Newfoundland with another convoy. There were sixty-two ships in the group, many of them tankers filled with high-octane aviation gas. Almost immediately we ran into a gale. The ships wallowed and floundered among mountainous waves. For nearly a week we had nothing to eat but sandwiches, and it was impossible to sleep. On top of this misery, we received an emergency alert and intelligence that the largest Nazi submarine wolf pack ever assembled was shadowing our convoy.

After a few days at sea, all grumbling and grousing stopped. We were too weary to do anything but stand watch-in-watch and strain our eyes and ears for the enemy. Finally the storm slackened and the submarines closed in. During the beginning of the second week, hardly a night went by without the sky lighting up with the explosions of torpedoed ships.

Then, at sunrise on the twenty-fifth of December, as we neared the southwest tip of Ireland, our protection arrived—Royal Navy planes. The seas calmed and we relaxed; for the first time in what had seemed ages, the men were able to get a hot meal and sleep.

All hands, except those on watch, turned in thankfully, exhausted.

Suddenly at nine o'clock on this Christmas morning, the bosun's mate piped reveille. A wave of grumbling passed over the ship. We had all expected to be able to sleep in unless there were an attack. A few minutes later Captain Stark's voice came over the loudspeaker. "This is the captain speaking. Shipmates, I know you are tired and want to sleep. But today is Christmas. There are special surprise packages from your families. They have been unloaded from the forward peak tanks and have been distributed throughout the ship alphabetically."

He went on to describe precisely where each group of presents was.

The news exploded through the ship. Men scrambled for their packages. Sailors sat all over the decks cutting string, tearing paper, wiping away tears, and shouting to shipmates about what they had received.

But the four Unholy K's found no presents. They stood together, watching the others sullenly.

"Christmas!" said Koenig. "That's only an excuse to get suckers to spend money."

"Don't show *me* your new wristwatch," sneered Krakow to a young sailor who proudly held it up. "If I need a new ticker, I'll buy me one."

One happy kid came jigging up with a huge box of fudge. "From my girl," he sang out. "Now I see why the Old Man wanted her name and address."

"Hey!" said Krakow, grabbing Kelly's arm. "Didn't we give the Old Man *our* girls' names and addresses?"

"Yeah," said Kratch, beginning to grin in a sly manner. "Rita Hayworth, Lana Turner, Paulette Goddard, and Ginger Rogers."

"Then how come we didn't get anything?"

"Let's go see the Old Man."

The Unholy K's, smiling evilly, went to the captain's cabin.

"Captain Stark, sir," said Krakow with mock respect, "we got a complaint. Everybody got presents from the names and addresses they gave you. . . ."

The captain looked at the four men gravely. "Don't you think that's pretty nice?"

"But we gave you names and addresses and we didn't get no presents."

"Oh, you didn't?" said the Old Man slowly.

"No, sir, everyone but us. That's discrimination, sir."

"By gum," said the captain, standing up, "there *are* four extra packages. Now I just wonder. . . ." He went to his bunk and pulled the blanket off a pile of parcels.

"There's one for me!" hollered Kelly, surging forward.

Captain Stark stood up to his full six feet and blocked the way. Reaching into the bunk, he handed out the packages to the four men, one at a time.

"Now, if you'll excuse me, I'll conduct yuletide services for all hands." He went out to the bridge.

The Unholy K's ripped the colored wrappings. Krakow couldn't open his fast enough and took his sheath knife to slash through the ribbon. Inside the fancy box was a pair of knitted woolen gloves. He tried them on his big red hands.

"Gee, the right size!"

There was something else in the box. It was a picture of a

shapely woman in a low-cut dress; and there was writing on it.

Dear Joe Krakow,

I knitted these gloves especially for you because you are my best boyfriend in the U.S. Navy. I hope that they'll keep you warm and that you'll have a wonderful Christmas wherever you may be.

From your best gal,
Rita Hayworth

Joe Krakow felt around his pockets for a handkerchief but couldn't find one. "What did you guys get?" he said, sniffling.

"Me," said Koenig shrilly, "I got a wallet and a picture of Paulette Goddard! *From Paulette Goddard!*"

Kelly received a wristwatch and an autographed picture from Ginger Rogers; and Kratch's present from Lana Turner was a gold fountain pen and a sentimentally inscribed photograph.

The Unholy K's shuffled around to the bridge where Captain Stark, his Bible open, stood in front of the microphone.

Krakow said, "Captain, sir. . . ."

"Later," the captain replied bluntly, without even turning. He switched on the loudspeaker system, announced church services, and read the story of the Nativity to all hands. Below in the engine room men listened, and in the chiefs' quarters, in the galley, in the mess compartments—throughout the entire ship two hundred and fifty sailors listened as the Old Man read the story of Jesus.

When he finished, he said he hoped everyone would join him in a few carols.

The Unholy K's pushed in on the captain. "Let us help you, sir," said Krakow urgently.

"This is not your type of song," the captain replied.

"Please, sir, the least we can do is lead the singing."

"Please, sir, let this be *our* Christmas present to *you*."

"A Christmas present for *me*?" mused the Old Man. "Why, yes, we'd all appreciate having a choir for the occasion. What shall we start with?"

The four sailors looked at the Old Man and then down at the photographs and presents clutched tightly under their arms. They gathered around the microphone. Krakow coughed; then in his deep bass he boomed, "Shipmates, this is Koenig, Kelly, Kratch, and me, Krakow—four no-good bums. Today is Christmas, and we want to sing you a special ballad." He paused, wiped his eyes and nose on his sleeve again.

Krakow raised his hand like a symphony conductor, and the quartet began to sing:

Silent night, holy night,
All is calm, all is bright . . .

The magic of the holy music spread. Everyone in the ship joined. The helmsman and the officer of the deck put their throats to the Christmas ballad. Even Captain Elias Stark, the granite man from New Hampshire, moved into the quartet, inclined his head and, in a reedy tenor, swelled the song.

Sleep in heavenly peace.
Sleep in heavenly peace.

The joyous music rose above the noise of the ocean and the

destroyer's engines. During the third stanza an enormous bird soared in from the low-hanging clouds and landed in the after rigging. It flapped its great wings and made noises as if it, too, were singing our Christmas ballad. My shipmates said it was an albatross. But, even though my eyes were filled with tears, I'd swear that it was an angel.

Of course, that was many years ago when I was still a kid. But even then I could recognize an angel when I saw one. As sure as my name's Joe Krakow.

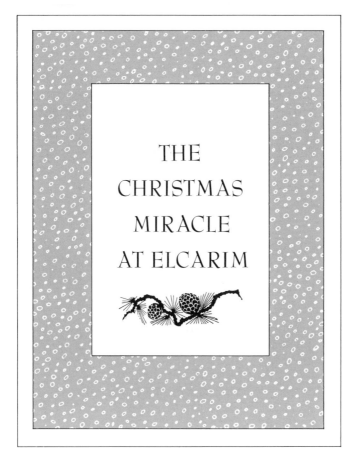

THE
CHRISTMAS
MIRACLE
AT ELCARIM

One of our sons, Bruce, was born in August. A few minutes after he was delivered, a firefly somehow got into the delivery room and flitted over Bruce, glowing brightly. One of the nurses joked. "Oh," she said, "it's just like the Star of Bethlehem."

Some years later, at church on Christmas Eve, we were reminded of the incident. The sermon was titled, "There Are a Million Stars of Bethlehem, One for Each of Us."

The minister spoke. "Everyone is born with a Star of Bethlehem shining over her or him. It comes in many forms. Perhaps it is a bright star in the sky, perhaps it is the sun, perhaps it is a neon light across the street, perhaps a solitary light bulb in the bedroom. It might even be a happy firefly."

He continued, "There is a Star of Bethlehem for each of us daily. It is very appropriate, then, that on this Christmas Eve we each begin looking for our daily star— regardless of its form; and accept it as God's daily miracle."

Upon returning from midnight service, the family (seeming to believe that I knew a lot about such matters) asked me to explain the phenomenon of everyone having a Star of Bethlehem.

I answered, paraphrasing our minister, "Oh, it's just another of God's miracles."

Brian asked, "Dad, what's a miracle?"

"I'll get the dictionary and look it up."

"No, Dad," interrupted Bruce, "Christmas Eve isn't the time for dictionaries. Tell us a story which illustrates a miracle, like, say, the Star of Bethlehem."

"C'mon, Dad, make up a story," said Jon.

Everyone else approved and so, then and there and a bit ramblingly, I made up and told the story of
The Christmas Miracle at Elcarim.

THE CHRISTMAS MIRACLE AT ELCARIM

 A long, long time ago there was a beautiful island named Elcarim. No people lived on Elcarim. However, there were animals, birds, insects. There were snakes, turtles, and frogs. There were grasses and flowers. But there were no people.

One day all the living things on the island had a meeting; and they agreed that they wanted to have either a king or a queen to rule over them. They desired a kingdom with a grand palace, with laws, with a fire department, taxes, and courts of justice. But they did not want any ordinary ruler. They wanted a king or a queen who could perform miracles.

The inhabitants of Elcarim decided to ask God for help. No one knows how, but somehow on a piece of birchbark, they wrote the following message:

> Dear Lord,
>> Please send us a ruler who can perform miracles.

They tied the bark to the leg of an eagle. The eagle flew up high into the air and disappeared in the white clouds.

Many, many months later the eagle returned, and tied to his leg was a piece of fine parchment, and on it was written:

My dear Residents of Elcarim,

About the time of the next new moon, a princess will come by ship to rule over you. She will be able to perform one *miracle. When this has been accomplished, she will make no others. But she will be wise, just, and beautiful.*

The next new moon was only a few days away.

The animals polished their claws, they brushed their fur, and cleaned their teeth. The birds preened their feathers and practiced their songs. The flowers put fresh paint on their petals and sprayed themselves with perfume. Everyone wanted to be pretty to please their new ruler. But a strange thing happened. In their hearts they suddenly grew greedy. Almost all of them had the same selfish thought: "Oh, perhaps she will do the one miracle for *me*."

The lions all thought, "I will please the princess and she will make for me a collar of gold; that is what I have always wanted."

The horses all thought, "Oh, I will please the princess and she will perform a miracle and make my hooves turn to silver."

The pigeons all thought, "Oh, I will please our new princess and she will make for me wings that shine in the sun like diamonds."

Almost everyone on the island selfishly was thinking, "How can I get this one miracle to be made *for me?*"

Well, then came the night when the new moon would shine brightly in the sky. It was the twenty-first of December, and it was time for the princess to arrive. Everyone knew that such an important person would come in a ship of gold, with sails made of gaily colored silk which would sparkle and dazzle. And the ship would sing as it cut through the blue waves. Everybody knew that the princess, in her majestic boat, would sail into the main harbor; and on the deck would be trumpeters in purple suits, announcing her arrival.

On the night of the new moon, all the animals and birds and insects—even the turtles—went down to the harbor. They brought good things to eat. They brought jewels, expensive gifts, and lovely things to please the princess.

During that evening, no golden ship came over the horizon. By sunrise the princess had not arrived. The next day passed and still there was no sign of her. Two more days went by. Still no princess.

The owl, who is a very wise fellow, said, "Ah, we have miscalculated her arrival and she will probably come during the night or maybe early tomorrow."

That night, on Christmas Eve, a storm arose, and no one could see the moon or stars. If the royal ship arrived it would be hidden in fog and rain. It would be tossing and jumping on great waves. The princess would have a difficult time coming ashore.

Each animal thought, *If I help her before the others, perhaps she will do the miracle for me.* They pushed and shoved and jostled each other to get close to the beach.

At midnight a pine tree on the top of the mountain cried, "Ship ahoy! Ship ahoy!"

"Where is it? Ah! Our princess has come!"

"Oh," said the pine tree, "it's around the bend—on the other side of the island. I can just barely see it in the rain. But it's a long way from the harbor."

Even though it was dark, and rainy, and windy, everybody ran to the other side of the island. As the lightning flashed, they saw the ship. It was not made of gold. It was not a big, regal ship, the kind a princess should come in. It was a tiny wooden fishing vessel with one stubby mast. A fishing boat! They knew, of course, that the princess wouldn't be on such a small and smelly craft. So they hurried back to the main harbor and built fires to keep themselves warm until their royal miracle worker should arrive.

There was one little insect who did not join them. He was a tiny bug—so insignificant that the animals never even talked to him. He shouted to the animals as loud as he could above the fierce storm, "There are people out there in the fishing craft. If we don't let them have a light, they'll be shipwrecked on the rocks."

But the animals were thinking only of the one miracle which the princess could perform. They wanted to be present when the princess came in, and they said, "No, no, the fishing boat is not important enough. There are a thousand fishing boats, but only one princess. She will be disappointed if we are not at the harbor to greet her."

Now a fog began covering the shoreline. The tiny insect felt very sorry for the poor people who would be shipwrecked. He decided to help the fishermen who were about to be cast up on the dangerous rocks, even though he knew he might not see the beautiful princess arrive. He went to the fire and picked up a small, burning twig in his legs. Oh how it burned! The flames singed him so badly that he could hardly rise off the ground. But he beat his wings very hard and managed to fly out in the storm toward the ship. He held the light over the rocks so that the people on the fishing boat would see the danger and not be smashed to death.

The fishermen saw the tiny beacon light of the brave little bug and they followed him to a small, safe harbor.

The next morning when the storm was over, the fishermen pulled up their anchor, hoisted their sail, and entered the main harbor. The animals waved them off and shouted, "Go away, go away, this is reserved for the princess and her golden boat." But the fishing boat came in anyhow.

When the small craft came up alongside the mooring rock, the hatch was opened and out stepped the princess. Her royal ship had been wrecked and the fishermen had rescued her.

The princess, oh, she was so beautiful! When she spoke, it sounded like nightingales singing. She said, "Gather around me."

The animals formed a circle close to her, thrusting their presents forward and shouting, "Here is my present for you! Here is *my* precious gift for you!"

When they were all seated she said, "Who held the light over the rocks last night and saved my life?"

No one answered. The brave little insect was not present. The insect who had brought the burning twig was dying. He had been so badly burned that he had fallen into the ocean and had been washed up on the other side of the island.

The wise princess said, "Where is my friend, the little insect?"

The animals did not know. Instead, they began to clutch at the princess' bejeweled gown and shout, "Do a miracle! Do a miracle!"

"Follow me," the princess said.

She went to the other side of the island. There, in the sand, was the little bug. The princess gently picked him up. "So you are the only one who was kind enough to help me," she said, "even though you didn't know that I was on the fishing boat."

The insect said, "Well, beautiful princess, to be truly kind, we must help everyone."

The princess smiled. "I can perform only one miracle. And I will do it now."

From her pocket she took a lovely diamond. It sparkled golden and silver and blue and red, like a great star. It was as bright as the Star of Bethlehem.

"This diamond I will give to you, dear insect. It will become part of you and it will shine and glow forever so that everyone will know that you are filled with love and goodness. And the diamond will pass to all of your sons and daughters."

The little bug took the precious jewel and it became part of him. Later his sons and daughters had ones exactly like it, just as the princess had said.

And now, at nighttime, you can see a million Stars of Bethlehem. Today the kindly insects are called fireflies or lightning bugs.

And that's the end of my story.

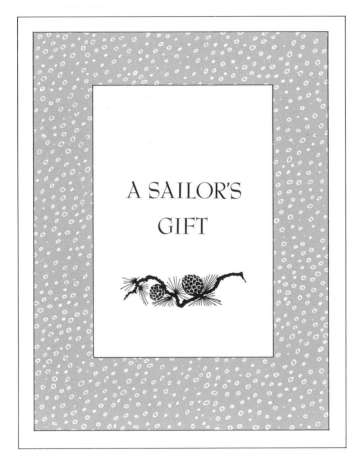

A SAILOR'S
GIFT

What prompted this tale?
Well, it explains itself.

A SAILOR'S GIFT

Admiral David L. McDonald, U.S.N.
Chief of Naval Operations
Washington 25, D.C.

Dear Admiral McDonald:

Eighteen people asked me to write this letter to you.

At Christmastime my wife, our three boys, and I were in France, on our way from Paris to Nice in a rented car. For five wretched days everything had gone wrong. On Christmas Eve, when we checked into our hotel in Nice, there was no Christmas spirit in our hearts.

It was raining and cold when we went out to eat. We found a drab little restaurant shoddily decorated for the holiday. Only five tables were occupied. There were two German couples, two French families, and an American sailor by himself. In the corner an old man listlessly played Christmas music on a battered piano.

I was too tired and miserable to care. I noticed that the other customers were eating in stony silence. The only person who seemed happy was the American sailor. While eating, he was writing a letter.

My wife ordered our meal in French. The waiter brought us the wrong thing. I scolded my wife for being stupid.

At the table with the French family on our left, the father slapped one of his children for some minor infraction, and the boy began to cry.

On our right, the German wife began berating her husband.

All of us were interrupted by an unpleasant blast of cold air. Through the front door came an old flower woman. She wore a dripping, tattered overcoat, and shuffled in on wet, rundown shoes. She went from one table to the other.

"Flowers, monsieurs, mesdames. Only one franc." No one bought.

Wearily she sat down at a table between the sailor and us. To the waiter she said, "A bowl of soup. I haven't sold a flower all afternoon." To the piano player she said hoarsely, "Can you imagine, Joseph, soup on Christmas Eve?"

He pointed to his empty "tipping plate."

The young sailor finished his meal and got up. Putting on his coat, he walked over to the flower woman's table.

"Happy Christmas," he said, smiling and picking out two corsages. "How much are they?"

"Two francs, monsieur."

Pressing one of the small corsages flat, he put it into the letter he had written, then handed the woman a twenty-franc note.

"I don't have change, monsieur," she said. "I'll get some from the waiter."

"No, ma'am," said the sailor, leaning over and kissing the ancient cheek. "This is my Christmas present to you."

Then he came to our table, holding the other corsage in front of him. "Sir," he said to me, "may I have permission to present these flowers to your beautiful daughter?"

In one quick motion he gave my wife the corsage, wished us a Merry Christmas, and departed. Everyone had stopped eating. Everyone had been watching the sailor.

A few seconds later Christmas exploded throughout the restaurant.

The old flower woman jumped up, waving the twenty-franc note, shouted to the piano player, "Joseph, my Christmas present! And you shall have half so you can have a feast, too."

The piano player began to belt out *O Holy Night.*

My wife waved her corsage in time to the music. She appeared ten years younger. She began to sing, and our three sons joined her, bellowing with enthusiasm.

"Gut! Gut!" shouted the Germans. They began singing in German.

The waiter embraced the flower woman. Waving their arms, they sang in French.

The Frenchman who had slapped the boy beat rhythm with his fork against a glass. The lad, now on his lap, sang in a youthful soprano.

A few hours earlier eighteen persons had been spending a miserable evening. It ended up being the happiest, the very best

Christmas Eve they had ever experienced.

This, Admiral McDonald, is what I am writing you about. As the top man in the navy, you should know about the very special gift that the U.S. Navy gave to my family, to me, and to the other people in that French restaurant. Because your young sailor had Christmas spirit in his soul, he released the love and joy that had been smothered within us by anger and disappointment. He gave us Christmas.

Thank you, sir, and Merry Christmas!

W. J. Lederer

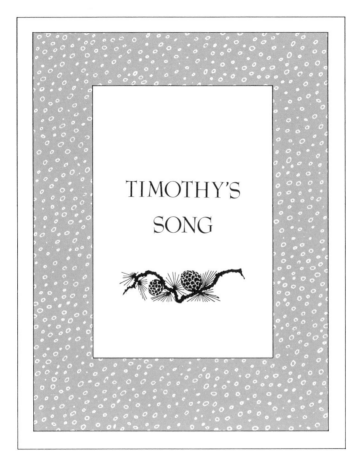

TIMOTHY'S
SONG

Bruce, Jon, and Brian all had read The Juggler of
Notre Dame. *This is a story of a very poor French juggler
who had no money to put into the church collection plate.
The only asset he had was his skill as a juggler—so he
stood before the altar and juggled for the glory of God. The
priests thought this was sacrilegious. But God thought
otherwise and a miracle was done.*

*When our Christmas Eve "story hour" came up at home,
the boys requested me to make up a story about "a kid in
America who did something similar to that of the poor
French juggler."*

*I recalled a young lad named Timothy whom I had
known many years ago in New York. He came to mind
because* The Juggler of Notre Dame *had been his favorite
story. Indeed, he sometimes fantasized himself as the
juggler.*

*Yes, I thought, I will tell my family about Timothy. I
had spent much time with Timothy. In fact, I had
witnessed almost every scene in this story. That is, every
scene except the last one. And, sometime in the future, I
may even witness that one.*

TIMOTHY'S SONG

Rain or snow, sleet or sun, Timothy the hunchback was at an out-of-the-way corner near Brooklyn Bridge, earning his living by selling newspapers. His face was tanned and lined from weather and hard work; his voice was deep and hoarse from shouting. He was eleven years old, although no one knew it, not even Timothy himself.

People came to Timothy and bought his papers partly because he was an odd-looking fellow. The clumsy, misproportioned little boy gave pleasure to his customers. No matter how hard times were, Timothy greeted everyone cheerfully. He carried packages for old ladies, led blind men across the street, and gave directions to lost strangers. Timothy loved animals; and three or four stray dogs followed the little hunchback wherever he went. He called them "my little brothers and sisters"; and with them he shared his meager sandwiches. He was happy when he helped others because when he did he heard wonderful music, and the whole world became more beautiful.

Timothy, who was not even five feet tall, wore men's cast-off clothing. The cutoff pants were frayed at the cuffs. His coat hung loosely, and his hands could scarcely reach into the pockets which were at his knees. But the oversized coat helped hide the hump on Timothy's back and drew attention away from his habit of walking with his head cocked to one side. He twisted his head because he had been born with weak eyes and partial deafness. He had to try very hard to see and hear.

Strangers often were startled by Timothy's unusual appearance. Once a woman looked at Timothy and said, "How alarming." This made him smile happily because he thought she had said, "How charming!"

Usually he had sold all his papers by seven o'clock at night; and then, with dogs following him, he walked to his room, which was in a garret next to a church. Several evenings a week, Timothy heard the church choir practicing, and he enjoyed it. In his tiny garret Timothy accompanied the choir. He sang loudly because he couldn't hear very well and because his voice had been made strong and hoarse from years of shouting "Paper!" When he sang, he felt big and glorious and important; and his heart overflowed with golden warmth. Sometimes the dogs joined him, barking and howling.

It seemed to Timothy that the people in the choir must, indeed, be angels. They must be, because their music was so heavenly. One cold day in December Timothy decided to find out. Leaving his garret, he went downstairs and slipped into the

side door of the church. From behind an empty pew, he watched
the choir practice.

Why, thought Timothy, *they are ordinary people no different from
me.*

For the next few days, when he was selling his papers and
shouting, "Read all about it! Extra! Extra!" he recalled the choir.
Even when the wind was bitterly cold and Timothy had to jump
up and down on his skinny, crooked legs to keep warm, he
thought of the choir members who sang so beautifully.

Perhaps, he thought, *I should join the choir. With a strong voice
like mine, the music will reach all the way to Heaven. Now is the time.
Christmas is only a few weeks away.*

He jigged joyously as he pictured himself with the others,
singing holy music.

He thought about it and thought about it; and then he made
up his mind. He *would* join the choir. That evening he walked
into the front door of the church and waited for the choir members to come for rehearsal. At eight o'clock they arrived, talking
and laughing along with their choirmaster and pastor. Many of
them were about Timothy's age. They wore fine clothes, and
Timothy heard them talk merrily about the Christmas presents
they hoped to receive.

Their pastor turned to Timothy. "What are you doing here,
my son?" he asked gently.

Ah, thought Timothy, *he called me his son. Surely he will be glad
when he learns that I have come to join the choir.*

In his rasping voice, Timothy said, "Sir, I have come to sing
for God."

[47]

"What can you sing?" asked the clergyman.

"Anything, sir. Anything at all," said Timothy, feeling proud that his voice was so loud. "From my window I can hear you practice. It is so beautiful. And when I hear the music, I sing the same melodies."

"Ah, you have a deep voice."

"Yes, sir. And I tell you, sir, people can hear me. I sell papers down by Brooklyn Bridge."

The young members of the choir smiled as they saw the misshapen little boy in his tattered clothes.

Ah, Timothy thought, *they are pleased that I have come to join them.*

"Come," said the pastor, "let's hear you sing."

The choir assembled and sheets of music were handed out. Timothy held his in front of him the way everyone else did; but because he did not see well, the notes were blurred; and no matter how hard he squinted he could not make them out. And of course, he couldn't read music anyway.

The choirmaster said, "We shall start."

The organ poured out its golden notes. The choir began to sing. Timothy opened his mouth and sang—but instead of music, a great noise like a foghorn came from his scarred throat.

The organ stopped. The choir stopped. A moment later the members were holding their hands to their mouths trying to keep back their laughter.

The pastor put his arm around Timothy and said, "My son, perhaps you need more training before you can sing in the choir. . . ."

"But, sir, I sing louder than any of them."

The pastor also forced back a smile.

"I know," he said. "But, my son, why don't you come to church and listen to the choir for a while and then you might learn more about it."

"I will be allowed to come here to church?"

"The Lord will welcome you."

This was one of the happiest moments of Timothy's life. He did not remember having a father or a mother, and he had been selling newspapers since he was eight years old. Never before had he been invited anyplace by anyone. The only school he had attended was one for the handicapped. At the school he had been taught to sell papers; and a small newsstand had been found for him near Brooklyn Bridge. Now he had been asked to come to church; and soon he would be in the choir singing to God.

On Sunday morning—the next day—he was at church early. The congregation trickled in. Everyone was dressed in Sunday clothes. As people passed the little hunchback with his raggedy, oversized clothes, they looked questioningly at him.

"Oh," thought Timothy, "they notice me. They are glad I am here."

The processional hymn began. Timothy heard it and the music swelled inside his heart. He opened his mouth to let the music out—loud, and filled with love for God. But when he began to sing, people around him turned and stared. His harsh unmusical voice startled them. Timothy thought they were applauding. He was happy and sang even louder. Almost everyone in the church turned to see what the commotion was.

A little girl in front of him turned to her mother and said, "Mommy, that boy's voice hurts my ears."

The pastor, who was at the end of the processional, saw what happened. He stopped by Timothy's pew. In a kindly manner he said, "My son, for the first few weeks, perhaps you should just listen. . . ."

It was then that Timothy knew that he could not sing, even though he heard wonderful songs in his heart. It was then he knew that his throat would never be able to make music. He realized that people were laughing at him, making fun of him because he was a misshapen little boy with a shrieking voice and a hunched back, a twisted body, and crooked little legs.

He ran from the church, weeping.

Timothy never returned; but, as always, when he was in his garret, he listened to the music of the organ and the choir. It was nearly Christmas, and the choir rehearsed hymns of joy and gladness.

As the lovely melodies floated upward, Timothy was puzzled. "But I hear music just like that in here," he said, tapping his heart. "I hear it when I feed the hungry dogs or when I help the blind men and the old ladies. Why will the music not come from my mouth as it comes from the mouths of others? If it does not come from my mouth, how will God hear me on Christmas morning?"

He tried many times to imitate the choir; but every time from his throat came a loud croaking, like that of a bullfrog. Even he recognized that he could not keep a tune.

It was now a few days before Christmas. In the streets, happy, merry people scurried home, their arms loaded with brightly colored packages, green holly, and cheerful red poinsettias. Radios played Christmas carols.

"At least," Timothy thought, "the music inside of me sounds just like those Christmas carols. If I could only sing them so that God could hear my inside music the way I hear it."

As he was sadly thinking about this, the skies became gray. The sun disappeared, and a bitter cold wind swept down from the north. It roared over the East River and around Brooklyn Bridge, bringing sleet and snow that covered Timothy's clothes with ice.

When he had sold his papers and fed his stray dogs, he returned home very, very tired. He could hardly hold his eyes open, and soon after he went to bed he felt hot; and he began to sneeze and cough.

The next day he fainted in the street. When he awakened, he was in a hospital. It was a charity hospital, and there were seventy-five beds in one ward, each bed very close to the next. The card on the foot of Timothy's bed said, "Pneumonia. Malnutrition." Even though he was very sick, Timothy saw that the other patients were old and poor and feeble and that there were only a few nurses and doctors to take care of the entire hospital.

When he heard patients moaning for water, or for a friend, or for assistance of any kind, he got out of bed and tried to help them. The little hunchback brought them water, straightened their beds, and gave them help if they wanted to move. These things made him happy, because with each act of kindness, he heard music in his heart. The more he helped others the more melodic was his inner music, the more beautiful became everything he saw.

Once again he tried to sing what was in his heart. He had hardly opened his mouth when the other patients shouted, "Stop that horrible roaring!"

From then on he stayed quiet.

"I guess it is best for me to listen," he said to himself. "Just the way the pastor told me."

On Christmas Eve the nurse found Timothy up, helping others. She noticed that his temperature had gone up and that he shook with spasms of coughing; and she scolded him and told him to stay under the blankets and not to leave his bed. But as soon as the nurse had gone, Timothy heard patients moaning. He stumbled from his bed again and continued trying to help those he believed were in need. And, ah, the good songs he heard! And how pretty the world was.

When it was almost midnight, just a few minutes before the day Jesus was born, Timothy felt very hot and very, very weak. Falling into his bed, he lay there with his eyes closed, wondering how long he would have to wait until the music in his heart could come out of his throat, so that he could sing to the glory of God.

Midnight came. The church bells played holy music to celebrate Christmas service. But Timothy did not hear them. His eyes were closed. He had stopped coughing.

When he opened his eyes, everything was clear. He could see perfectly. He did not have to squint. All around him were green hills and meadows. They were bright with yellow daffodils, white calla lilies, and red poinsettias.

Behind him, Timothy heard voices. They were soft and gentle, but he heard every small sound effortlessly. No longer did he have to cup his ear and twist his head to understand what people were saying.

Turning in the direction of the gentle voices, he saw a golden light. On both sides of the light stood many angels. Timothy was surprised. There were all kinds of angels. Some were seven feet tall. Some were medium-sized. Some were old, some young. Some were fat, some were thin. There even were hunchbacked angels with skinny, crooked legs. All of them smiled happily. Everything was beautiful—just the way the earth had been whenever Timothy did loving kind acts for others.

One of the tall angels stepped forward. "Welcome to Heaven, Timothy. We are glad you are here."

Timothy was afraid to talk. He was frightened lest his loud voice would spoil everything; and he answered by nodding his head.

The tall angel stretched forth his hand and said, "The Lord wishes that you will sing for Him again."

Timothy did not reply.

The angel repeated, "Timothy, God commands that you sing for Him again."

Filled with shame and panic, Timothy thought, *Ah, even here they mock me.*

He whispered to the angel, "I cannot sing. For me it is better to listen."

Desperately, little Timothy continued, "But, oh, let me stay here. There are many other things I can do. I can sell papers. I can shine shoes. I can help old people. I can feed hungry dogs. I can make beds. And if there's a hospital up here I can do chores."

He heard a gentle voice say, "It is My wish, Timothy, that you sing again for Me here, as you already have sung for Me on earth."

Timothy got on his knees and pleaded, "Lord God, I am Timothy the newsboy. I sell papers by Brooklyn Bridge. When I try to sing, people laugh at me. They think it is like the croaking of a frog, like a ship in the fog, like . . ."

Timothy was interrupted by thunder and a flash of lightning. A white cloud formed, and on the cloud stood a group of children. Timothy saw them clearly. It was the choir he had tried to join. Standing among the singers was an ugly little boy with a hump on his back. He recognized the boy as himself.

"Yes, Lord, that's me all right," said Timothy, wiping his eyes on his sleeve.

An angel pointed to the choir and told Timothy to listen.

The choir—with Timothy standing in the middle—began to sing. There was the choirmaster standing in front, keeping time with his hand. Timothy watched with horror as the ugly little dwarf squinted at the sheet of music and opened his mouth to sing.

He knew what would come next—his rasping, bellowing, croaking voice. He cringed and braced himself for the taunting laughter of the angels.

Then a strange thing happened. The dwarf's mouth began to move, but no horrible screeches came from it. Instead, from the crooked mouth came beautiful music. It sounded like ten wonderful choirs.

"Why, Lord," Timothy said, as the choir disappeared, "there

is a mistake. That's not the noise I made. That is the music I have in my heart."

The gentle but mighty Voice said, "My son, in your heart you sang for Me. I heard it here in Heaven. I heard it often, and it was good."

The angels came forward and lifted Timothy from his knees.

He no longer was afraid. He felt safe and at home. Heaven was just as beautiful as earth when Timothy had done loving things for others. The music in his heart swelled with joy. He could not hold it in. He opened his mouth to sing, and from his mouth came golden notes—loud, clear, and beautiful.

"Come close to Me," said the Voice, "and do not stop singing. Your songs—which are good deeds that come from the heart—they are the melodies I love best of all."

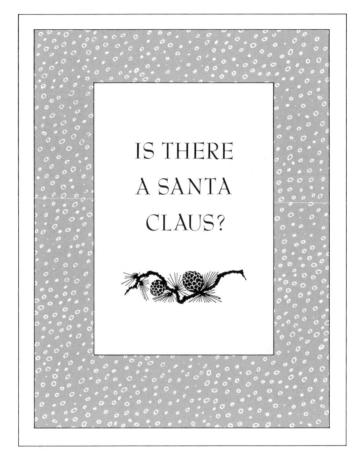

IS THERE
A SANTA
CLAUS?

IS THERE A SANTA CLAUS?

6 P.M., *December 23*

 I am writing this on the plane from New York to Los Angeles. We are in bad weather. The plane bumps up and down. The visibility is zero. The passengers are nervous; almost every one of them is going home for Christmas. Most of them have to connect in Los Angeles with other flights. That includes me. My flight to Honolulu and home departs at 10 P.M.

But I have another problem. When I get home to Honolulu tomorrow, I must have a Christmas story ready to tell the neighborhood children. They have asked me to title it, "How do I *know* there's a Santa Claus?" I believe they're pulling my leg. The youngsters are seven to sixteen years old. They're smart and skeptical.

8:10 P.M.

The pilot has just given us bad news. Los Angeles is fogged in; no aircraft can land. We have to detour to Ontario, California, an emergency field not far from Los Angeles.

3:12 A.M., *December 24*

The sun hasn't risen yet. It's dark, damp, and chilly. What with one problem and another, we have just landed in Ontario, California—six hours behind schedule. Everyone is cold, exhausted, hungry, and irritable. All of us on the plane will miss our connections. Many will not make it home tonight in time for Christmas Eve. I am in no mood to make up a story about Santa Claus even though I had promised the children.

I wonder when we'll get out of this emergency field at Ontario. What a mess! Santa Claus? Bah! Humbug!

7:15 A.M., *December 24*

I am writing this at the Los Angeles airport, having just arrived here by bus from Ontario.

A lot has happened in the last four hours. The airfield at Ontario, where we made an emergency landing about 3 A.M., was a bedlam. Many Los Angeles–bound planes had to land there. The frantic passengers—it seems like several thousand of them— had hoped to get word to their families that they would be late— and might not make it home for Christmas Eve. But the telegraph office was closed, and there were endless lines at the three telephone booths. No food. No coffee.

The employees at the small terminal were just as frenzied and fatigued as the passengers. Everything had gone wrong. Baggage was heaped helter-skelter, regardless of destination. No one knew which buses would go where, or at what time. Babies were crying, women were shouting questions, men were bellowing commands to which no one paid attention. In the effort to find luggage, the mob swarmed and jostled like an army of frightened ants. People shoved each other, swore, and complained. The loudspeakers crackled and blared announcements which were difficult to understand.

It hardly seemed possible that this was the day of Christmas Eve.

Suddenly, amid the nervous commotion, I heard a confident, unhurried voice. It stood out like a great church bell—clear, calm, and filled with love.

"Now don't you worry, ma'am," the voice said. "We're going to find your luggage and get you to La Jolla in time. Everything's going to be just fine."

This was the first positive, constructive statement I had heard since landing.

I turned and saw a man who might have stepped right out of "The Night before Christmas." He was short and stout, with a florid, merry face. On his head was some sort of official cap, the kind that sightseeing guides wear. Tumbling out beneath were cascades of curly white hair. He wore hiking boots, as if, perhaps, he had just arrived after a snowy trip behind a team of reindeer. Pulled snugly over his barrel chest and fat tummy was a red sweatshirt.

The man stood next to a homemade pushcart, composed of an

enormous packing box resting on four bicycle wheels. It contained urns of steaming coffee and piles of miscellaneous cardboard cartons.

"Here you are, ma'am," said the roly-poly man with the red sweatshirt and the cheerful voice. "Have some hot coffee while we look for your luggage."

Pushing the cart before him, pausing only long enough to hand coffee to others, or to say a cheerful "Merry Christmas to you, brother!" or to promise that he would be back to help, he searched among the sprawling piles of luggage. Finally he found the woman's possessions. Placing them on the pushcart, he said to her, "You just follow me. We'll put you on the bus to La Jolla."

After getting her settled, Kris Kringle (that's what I had started calling him) returned to the terminal. I found myself tagging along and helping him with the coffee. I knew that my bus wouldn't leave for a while yet.

Kris Kringle stood out like a beam of light in that murky, noisy, dismal field. There was something about him that made everyone smile. Dispensing coffee, blowing a child's nose, laughing, singing snatches of Christmas songs, he calmed panicky passengers and sped them on their way.

When a woman fainted, it was Kris Kringle who pushed through the helpless group around her. From one of his cartons he produced smelling salts and a blanket. When the woman was conscious again, he asked three men to carry her into the terminal building and told them to use the loudspeaker system to find a doctor.

I wondered, Who is this funny, stout little man who gets things done?

I asked him, "What company do you work for?"

"Sonny," he said to me, "see that kid over there in the blue coat? She's lost. Give her this candy bar, and tell her to stay right where she is. If she wanders around, her mother won't ever find her."

I did as ordered, then repeated, "What company do you work for?"

"Shucks, I'm not working for anyone. I'm just having fun. Every December I spend my two weeks' vacation helping travelers. What with this rush season there is always somebody who needs a hand. Hey, look what we have over here."

He had spotted a tearful young mother with a baby. Winking at me, Kris Kringle perked his cap at a jaunty angle and rolled his cart over to them. The woman was sitting on her suitcase, clutching her child.

"Well, well, sister," he said, "that's a mighty pretty baby you have. What's the trouble?"

Between sobs, the young woman told him that she hadn't seen her husband for over a year. She was to meet him at a hotel in San Diego. He wouldn't know what had delayed her, and would worry. And the baby was hungry.

From the pushcart Kris Kringle took a bottle of warmed milk. "Now don't you worry. Everything will be all right."

As he guided her to the bus for Los Angeles—the one I was to leave on—he wrote in his notebook her name and the name of the hotel in San Diego. He helped her onto the bus and promised her that he would get a message to her husband.

"God bless you," she said, making herself comfortable and cradling the now sleeping child in her arms. "I hope you have a merry Christmas and many wonderful presents."

"Thank you, sister," he said, tipping his cap. "I've already received the greatest gift of all, and you gave it to me. Oh, oh," he said, looking out the bus window. "There's an old fellow in trouble. Good-bye, sister. I'm going over there and give myself another present."

He got off the bus. I got off, too, since the bus wouldn't leave for a few minutes. He turned to me.

"Say," he said, "aren't you taking this jalopy to Los Angeles?"

"Yes."

"Okay, you've been a good assistant. Now I want to give *you* a Christmas present. You sit next to that lady and look after her and the baby. When you get to Los Angeles"—he tore a piece of paper from his notebook—"telephone her husband at this hotel in San Diego. Tell him about his family's delay."

He knew what my answer would be, because he left without even waiting for a reply. I sat down next to the young mother, took the baby from her. Looking out the window, I saw Kris Kringle in his bulging red sweatshirt disappearing into the crowd.

The bus started. I felt good. I began thinking of home and Christmas. And I knew then how I would answer the question of the children in my neighborhood: "How do I *know* there's a Santa Claus?"

How do I know there's a Santa Claus? Gracious, friends, I've met him!